I'm
MAD
at you

I'm *MAD* at you

Verses selected by William Cole

Illustrations by GEORGE MacCLAIN

Collins

Library of Congress Cataloging in Publication Data
Main entry under title: I'm mad at you.
Summary: A collection of poems from a variety of sources describing and
expressing a range of angry thoughts from pique to rage.
1. Anger—Juvenile poetry. [1. Anger—poetry. 2. American poetry—
Collections.] I. Cole, William, 1919-   II. MacClain, George.
PN6110.C4144   1978   811'.008'0353   77-25497
ISBN 0-529-05363-2

COPYRIGHT ACKNOWLEDGMENTS

Collins Publishers would like to thank the following authors, publishers, and agents whose interest, co-operation, and permission to reprint have made possible the preparation of *I'm Mad at You*. All possible care has been taken to trace the ownership of every selection included and to make full acknowledgment for its use. If any errors have accidentally occurred, they will be corrected in subsequent editions, provided notification is sent to the publishers.

"I Hate Harry" by Miriam Chaikin. Copyright © 1978 by Miriam Chaikin. By permission of the author and McIntosh and Otis, Inc.

"Don't You Dare" from *And the Frog Went "Blah!"* by Arnold Spilka, copyright © 1972; "A Little Girl I Hate" from *A Rumbudgin of Nonsense* by Arnold Spilka, copyright © 1970; "Puzzle" from *A Lion I Can Do Without* by Arnold Spilka, copyright © 1964. Reprinted by permission of Frances Schwartz Literary Agency.

"Katawumpus" and "Good and Bad" by Edward Abbott Parry from *Katawumpus*. Reprinted by permission of Anthony Sheil Associates, Ltd.

"Anger" by Yvonne Lowe from the *Daily Mirror* Children's Literature Competition. Reprinted by permission of the *Daily Mirror*.

"The Worst" and "If I Had a Firecracker" by Shel Silverstein. Reprinted by permission of the author.

"Dan Dunder" and "What Someone Said When He Was Spanked on the Day Before His Birthday" from *You Read to Me, I'll Read to You* by John Ciardi. Copyright © 1962 by John Ciardi. "Someone's Face" from *The Man Who Sang the Sillies* by John Ciardi. Copyright © 1961 by John Ciardi. Reprinted by permission of J. B. Lippincott Company.

"Mean Song" from *There Is No Rhyme for Silver* by Eve Merriam. Copyright © 1962 by Eve Merriam. "Crosspatch" from *All the Day Long* by Nina Payne. Text copyright © 1973 by Nina Payne. Used by permission of Atheneum Publishers.

"Nomenclature" from *The Ombley-Gombley* by Peter Wesley-Smith. Copyright © 1969 by Peter Wesley-Smith and David Fielding. Used by permission of Atheneum Publishers and Angus and Robertson Publishers, Sydney.

Contents

I'M SO MAD I COULD SCREAM!

I'm so mad I could scream,
I'm so mad I could spit,
Turn over a table,
Run off in a snit!

I'm so mad I could yell,
I could tear out my hair,
Throw a rock through a window,
Or wrestle a bear!

I mean—I am furious,
In a terrible huff,
I'm raging and roaring
And boy, am I tough!

I'm really ferocious,
I really am *mad*,
I'm ready to beat up
My mother and dad!

On thinking it over,
I *will not* leave home,
But I'll put all my anger
Right here in this poem.

I'm feeling much better—
Like peaches and cream—
For a poem is the best way
Of letting off steam!

WILLIAM COLE

IF I HAD A FIRECRACKER

If I had a firecracker
Twelve feet high,
And taller than fifteen men,
I'd set it off on the Fourth of July
And blow Lucille twelve miles high
So she wouldn't come down till *next* July.
And then I'd do it again.

SHEL SILVERSTEIN

DAN DUNDER

Dan Dunder is a blunder.
What makes Dan so loud, I wonder?
If *I* knew how to be that loud
I think I'd look for a big black cloud
And get a job with it—as thunder!

JOHN CIARDI

WHAT SOMEONE SAID WHEN HE WAS SPANKED
ON THE DAY BEFORE HIS BIRTHDAY

Some day
I may
Pack my bag and run away.
Some day
I may.
—But not today

Some night
I might
Slip away in the moonlight.
I might
Some night
—But not tonight.

Some night
Some day.
I might
I may
—But right now I think I'll stay.

JOHN CIARDI

GOD MADE THE RIVERS

God made the rivers,
God made the lakes,
God made you.
We all make mistakes.

AUTOGRAPH VERSE

TEN KINDS

Winnie Whiney, all things grieve her;
Fannie Fibber, who'd believe her?
Lotty Loozem, late to school, sir;
Albert Allplay, quite a fool, sir;
Kitty Kissem, loved by many,
George Grump, not loved by any;
Ralph Ruff,—beware his fist, sir;
Tillie Tattle, like a blister;
Gus Goodactin, bright and cheery;
Sammy Selfish, sour and dreary.
Do you know them, as I've sung them?
Easy 'tis to choose among them.

MARY MAPES DODGE

KING'S CROSS

King's Cross.
What shall we do?
His purple robe
Is rent in two!
Out of his crown
He's torn the gems!
He's thrown his scepter
Into the Thames!
The Court is shaking
In its shoe.
King's Cross
What shall we do?
Leave him alone for a minute or two.

ELEANOR FARJEON

GROW UP

Grow up, grow up.
Every time I look at you
I throw up

AUTOGRAPH VERSE

"What's the horriblest thing you've seen?"
Said Nell to Jean.

"Some gray-colored, trodden-on plasticine;
On a plate, a left-over cold baked bean;
A cloak-room ticket numbered thirteen;
A slice of meat without any lean;
The smile of a spiteful fairy-tale queen;

16

A thing in the sea like a brown submarine;
A cheese fur-coated in brilliant green;
A bluebottle perched on a piece of sardine.
What's the horriblest thing you've seen?"
Said Jean to Nell.

"Your face, as you tell
Of all the horriblest things you've seen."

ROY FULLER

17

CRY-BABY

A cry-baby whimpers wherever she goes.
She cries if a pussycat steps on her toes,
Or a ladybug lights on the end of her nose.
    Boohoo! Boohoo! Boohoo!

A cry-baby weeps if she can't have her way.
She screams and she yells for the rest of the day.
She'd much rather whine than dine or play.
    Boohoo! Boohoo! Boohoo!

A cry-baby sobs if her mother says "No—
You cannot stay up for a late TV show.
It's past nine o'clock—to bed you must go."
    Boohoo! Boohoo! Boohoo!

The least little thing makes a cry-baby bawl,
Like bumping her knee on a chair in the hall.
Indeed, she will wail over nothing at all.
    Boohoo! Boohoo! Boohoo!

MARTIN GARDNER

FIVE LITTLE PIGGIES

My Little
dad
had
five little piggies:
good 'un,
bad 'un,
gay 'un,
sad 'un,
and one little piggie
who was
mad
    mad
      mad!
Five little piggies
had
my little
dad.

DANISH NURSERY RHYME
Translated by N.M. Bodecker

MEAN SONG

Snickles and podes,
Ribble and grodes:
That's what I wish you.

A nox in the groot,
A root in the stoot
And a gock in the forbeshaw, too.

Keep out of sight
For fear that I might
Glom you a gravely snave.

Don't show your face
Around any place
Or you'll get one flack snack in the bave.

EVE MERRIAM

NUTS TO YOU, AND NUTS TO ME!

Nuts to you, and nuts to me!
Walnut, chestnut, hickory,
Butter-, coco-, hazel-, pea-
Nuts to you and nuts to me!

MARY ANN HOBERMAN

THE OUTLAW

Into the house of a Mrs. MacGruder
Came a very big outlaw
With a real six-shooter,
And he kicked the door
With his cowboy boot
And he searched the place
For valuable loot,

And he didn't take off his cowboy hat
But he quickly unlimbered his cowboy gat
And he cocked the gun
And he took his aim
And he called that Mrs. MacG by name
And he said in a terrible outlaw drawl,
"Git me that cake . . . and git it all!"

And Mrs. MacGruder patted his head,
"You may have a slice with some milk," she said.

FELICE HOLMAN

BICKERING

The folks in Little Bickering
they argue quite a lot.
Is tutoring in bickering
required for a tot?
Are figs the best for figuring?
Is pepper ice cream hot?
Are wicks the best for wickering
a wicker chair or cot?
They find this endless dickering
and nonsense and nit-pickering
uncommonly invigor'ing,
I find it downright sickering!
You do agree!
Why not?

N. M. BODECKER

THE WAY TO THE ZOO

That's the way to the zoo,
That's the way to the zoo,
The monkey house is nearly full
But there's room enough for you.

CHILDREN'S STREET RHYME

KATHERINE TATTLES

When Kate and Karen
Have their battles,
Katherine tattles.

When Kay and Katherine
Have a spat,
Kate tells that.

When Katherine and Kate
Their tempers lose,
Kay spreads the news.

But Karen gets
The greatest glory.
She turns a friendly fight
Into a full-length story,
And makes it gory.

LELAND B. JACOBS

YOU WERE THE MOTHER LAST TIME

"You were the mother last time.
It's my turn today."
　　"It's *my* turn."
"No, *my* turn."
　　"All right then, I won't play."
"Oh, go ahead then, *be* the mother.
It's not fair
But I don't care."

"I was the father last time.
I won't be today."
　　"It's your turn."
"No, *your* turn."
　　"All right then, I won't play."
"Oh, never mind, *don't* be the father.
It's not fair
But I don't care."

"I was the sister last time.
It's your turn today."
        "It is not."
"It is so."
        "All right then, I won't play."
"Oh, never mind, *don't* be the sister.
It's not fair
But I don't care."

"I have an idea!
Let's *both* be mothers!
(We'll pretend
About the others.)"

MARY ANN HOBERMAN

MAGIC WORD

"More jam," said Rosie to her Mom.
"I want more jam," said she.
    But no one heard
    The Magic Word.
Mom took a sip of tea.

"The jam! The jam! The jam!" she cried.
Her voice rang loud and clear.
    "I'd like to spread
    It on my bread."
But no one seemed to hear.

"*Please* pass the jam," Rose said at last.
Now *that's* the thing to say.
    When Mother heard
    The Magic Word
She passed it right away.

MARTIN GARDNER

IMPETUOUS SAMUEL

Sam had spirits naught could check,
    And today, at breakfast, he
Broke his baby sister's neck,
    So he shan't have jam for tea!

HARRY GRAHAM

DON'T YOU DARE!

Don't tell me that I talk too much!
Don't say it!
Don't you dare!
I only say important things
Like why it's raining where.
Or when or how or why or what
Might happen here or there.
And why a thing is this or that
And who is bound to care.
So don't tell me I talk too much!
Don't say it!
DON'T YOU DARE!

ARNOLD SPILKA

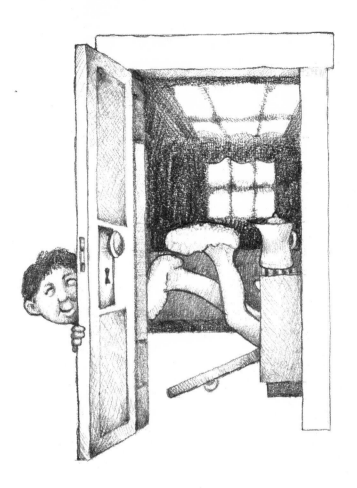

MOTHER'S NERVES

My mother said, "If just once more
I hear you slam that old screen door,
I'll tear out my hair! I'll dive in the stove!"
I gave it a bang and in she dove.

X. J. KENNEDY

I WOKE UP THIS MORNING

I woke up this morning
At quarter past seven.
I kicked up the covers
And stuck out my toe.
And ever since then
(That's a quarter past seven)
They haven't said anything
Other than "no."
They haven't said anything
Other than "Please, dear,
Don't do what you're doing,"
Or "Lower your voice."
Whatever I've done
And however I've chosen,
I've done the wrong thing
And I've made the wrong choice.
I didn't wash well
And I didn't say thank you.
I didn't shake hands
And I didn't say please
I didn't say sorry
When passing the candy,

I banged the box into
Miss Witelson's knees.
I didn't say sorry.
I didn't stand straighter.
I didn't speak louder
When asked what I'd said.
Well, I said
That tomorrow
At quarter past seven
They can
Come in and get me.
I'm Staying In Bed.

KARLA KUSKIN

TONY BALONEY

Tony Baloney is fibbing again—
Look at him wiggle and try to pretend.
Tony Baloney is telling a lie:
Phony old Tony Baloney, goodbye!

DENNIS LEE

GOD MADE THE FRENCH

God made the French,
God made the Dutch,
Whoever made you
Never made much.

CHILDREN'S STREET RHYME

HERE I AM

Here I am, bully,
    Chicken yellow.
I won't fight you.
The last thing to do
Is fight you
With your big red fists and fat cheeks
And mouth like a bursted balloon.

MYRA COHN LIVINGSTON

ANGER

I was angry and mad,
And it seemed that there was hot water inside me,
And as I got madder and madder,
The water got hotter and hotter all the time,
I was in a rage,

Then I began to see colors,
Like black and red,
Then as I got madder and madder,
My eyes began to pop out of my head,
They were popping up and down,
It was horrible,
And it would not stop,
I was steaming with anger,
Nobody could not stop me,
My mother could not stop me,
Then it was gone,
And I was all right,
Horrible, black, madness.

YVONNE LOWE, age 8

JUG AND MUG

"Jug, aren't you fond of Mug?"
"Him I could hug," said Jug.
"Mug, aren't you fond of Jug?"
"Him I could almost slug!"
"Humph," said Jug with a shrug.
"When he pours, he goes *Glug!*" said Mug.
"Well, *I* don't spill on the rug," said Jug.
"Smug old Jug," said Mug.
"I'll fill you, Mug," said Jug.
"*Will*, will you, Jug!" said Mug.
"Don't be ugly," said Jug juggly.
"But lug," said Mug.
 Glug.

DAVID McCORD

TIGER

I'm a tiger
Striped with fur
Don't come near
Or I might Grrr
Don't come near
Or I might growl
Don't come near
Or I might
BITE!

MARY ANN HOBERMAN

KATAWUMPUS

When little girls or little boys,
Set out to do just what they like,
Tear picture-books and smash their toys
And cry and howl and kick and strike,
Poor parents wonder what they're at,
Of course—they've got a fit of Kat-
                          a-wumpus.

If you have the Katawumpus
You feel rather like a grumpus
When the homeward tide is southerly and slack;
Horrid pains in every scale,
And a headache in your tail,
While barnacles are creeping up your back.

When children will not go to bed,
Or cry because they're asked to sing,
You'd think, to see the tears they shed,
The little things were suffering,
The symptoms are so various that
'Tis hard to know what is not Kat-
                                    a-wumpus.

When every other word they utter
Is either "shan't" or "pig" or "don't,"
And if when offered bread and butter
They snarl or pout or say "I won't,"
If they refuse to eat up fat,
'Tis certain it's a fit of Kat-
                                    a-wumpus.

EDWARD ABBOTT PARRY

41

GOOD AND BAD

Children are as good as gold
Or else as bad as blacking.
The first nice stories should be told,
The others want a thwacking.

Though sometimes they are rude and wild,
'Tis honester to own up
I've never known a naughty child
As naughty as a grown-up.

EDWARD ABBOTT PARRY

BROTHER

I had a little brother
And I brought him to my mother
And I said I want another
Little brother for a change.

But she said don't be a bother
So I took him to my father
And I said this little bother
Of a brother's very strange.

But he said one little brother
Is exactly like another
And every little brother
Misbehaves a bit he said.

So I took the little bother
From my mother and my father
And I put the little bother
Of a brother back to bed.

MARY ANN HOBERMAN

CROSSPATCH

Leave me alone
to mend my ouches.

I'm overgrown
by grumps and grouches.

I want to weed
my thorns and thistles.

The wind grows wild
before it whistles.

I can't rain
until I thunder.

I'll sow new seeds
when my crust turns under.

NINA PAYNE

ON THE BEHAVIOR OF RODNEY IV
WHO TRAVELS IN UNUSUAL CONTRAPTIONS

When he's riding
In a dirigible,
Rodney's behavior
Is incorrigible

(& you should see
The little imp
When he travels
In a blimp!)

For Rodney
Has a silver pin
To puncture holes
Within the skin—

When gas goes Phffft,
Dirigibles burst.
Rodney's behavior
Could not be worse.

LOUIS PHILLIPS

THE VISITOR

it came today to visit
and moved into the house
it was smaller than an elephant
but larger than a mouse

first it slapped my sister
then it kicked my dad
then it pushed my mother
oh! that really made me mad

it went and tickled rover
and terrified the cat
it sliced apart my necktie
and rudely crushed my hat

it smeared my head with honey
and filled the tub with rocks
and when i yelled in anger
it stole my shoes and socks

that's just the way it happened
it happened all today
before it bowed politely
and softly went away

JACK PRELUTSKY

MIND YOUR OWN BUSINSS

Mind your own business,
Fry your own fish;
Don't poke your nose
Into my clean dish.

CHILDREN'S STREET RHYME

STICKS AND STONES

Sticks and stones
Will break my bones
But names will never hurt me;

When you're dead
And in your grave
You'll pay for what
You called me.

TRADITIONAL RHYME
(IRISH VERSION)

THE HOWLERY GROWLERY ROOM

It doesn't pay to be cross,
It's not worth while to try it;
For Mammy's eyes so sharp
Are very sure to spy it:
A pinch on Billy's arm,
A snarl or a sudden gloom,
No longer we stay, but must up and away
To the Howlery Growlery Room.

Chorus

Hi! the Howlery! ho! the Growlery!
Ha! the Sniffery, Snarlery, Scowlery!
There we may stay,
If we choose, all day;
But it's only a smile that can bring us away.

If Mammy catches me
A-pitching into Billy;
If Billy breaks my whip,
Or scares my rabbit silly,
It's "Make it up, boys, quick!
Or else you know your doom!"
We must kiss and be friends, or the squabble ends
In the Howlery Growlery Room.

Chorus

Hi! the Howlery! ho! the Growlery! *etc*.

So it doesn't pay to be bad,
There's nothing to be won in it;
And when you come to think,
There's really not much fun in it.
So, come! the sun is out,
The lilacs are all a-bloom;
Come out and play, and we'll keep away
From the Howley Growlery Room.

Chorus

Hi! the Howlery! ho! the Growlery! *etc*.

LAURA E. RICHARDS

I HATE HARRY

I hate Harry like...like...OOO!
I hate Harry like...GEE!
I hate that Harry like—poison.
I hate! hate! hate! HAR-RY!

Rat! Dope! Skunk! Bum! Liar!
Dumber than the dumbest dumb flea!
BOY!...do I hate Harry,
I hate him the most that can be.

I hate him a hundred, thousand, million
Doubled, and multiplied by three,
A skillion, trillion, zillion more times
Than Harry, that rat, hates me.

MIRIAM CHAIKIN

MYRTLE

There once was a girl named Myrtle
Who, strangely enough, was a Turtle:
She was mad as a Hare,
She could growl like a Bear—
O *No*body understood Myrtle!

She would sit with a book on her Knees—
My Poetry Book, if you please—
She'd Rant and She'd Roar:
"This stuff is a Bore!
Why I could do better
With only ONE Letter—
These Poets, they write like *I* Sneeze!

THEODORE ROETHKE

FATHER SAYS

Father says
Never
let
me
see
you
doing
that
again
father says
tell you once
tell you a thousand times
come hell or high water
his finger drills my shoulder
never let me see you doing that again

My brother knows all his phrases off by heart
so we practice them in bed at night.

MICHAEL ROSEN

THE WORST

They say that I'm mean cause I spit and I scream
And I'm nasty and rasty and mad.
But I've looked at myself and I've looked at the rest
And there's so many good folks what's one more or less,
So if I can't be the best of the best
Then I'll be the worst of the bad.

SHEL SILVERSTEIN

SULKY SUE

Here's Sulky Sue;
What shall we do?
Turn her face to the wall
Till she comes to.

ENGLISH NURSERY RHYME

BAD BOY'S SWAN SONG

Evening waddles over the fields like a turkey.
　　　　　　　　　　　—JAMES REANEY

Evening waddles over the fields like a turkey,
　　And I, for one, have really cooked my goose—
I who started the day out fresh and perky,
　　Feeling on top of the world, all fast and loose.

I took apart my sister's pretty wagon
　　And stuffed the parts (by mistake) down the laundry chute,
Then wrapped the box back up, put ribbon and tag on,
　　So when she opens it up she'll scream, "You brute!"

When Father returns in a little while from work, he
　　Will surely blow his top—just my bad luck.
Evening waddles over the fields like a turkey;
　　And I'm a gone gosling, yes, sir, a real dead duck.

WILLIAM JAY SMITH

A LITTLE GIRL I HATE

I saw a little girl I hate
And kicked her with my toes.
She turned
And smiled
And KISSED me!
Then she punched me in the nose.

ARNOLD SPILKA

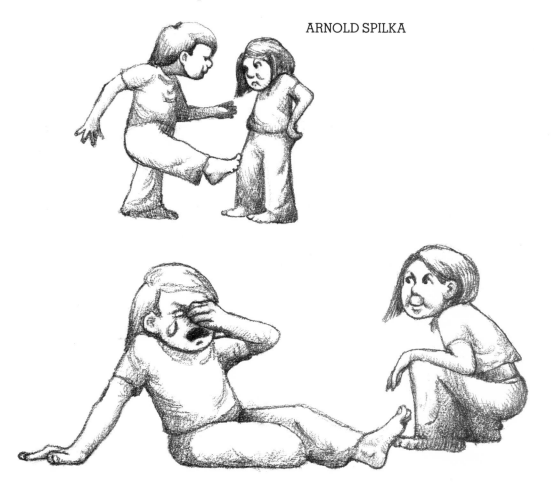

PATSY DOOLIN

When I am bad, my father gets
A voice he likes to fool in
And says to me:
"Who's that I see?
It must be Patsy Doolin."
This Patsy Doolin's not a type
That fathers find delightful.
She hates to eat
And kicks her feet
And fusses something frightful.

But when my father tells her, "GO!"
And frowns and shakes his head.
She takes her tears
And disappears,
And I come back instead.
At last my father sees the change
And sort of starts in humming
And says to me
Quite honestly
He hopes she won't keep coming.

My older sisters told me once
Their lives were just the same.
When they were small
And fussed and all,
Then Patsy Doolin came.
But since my father *hates* a house
That no one minds a rule in.
They worked like me
And finally
They drove out Patsy Doolin.

KAYE STARBIRD

NOMENCLATURE

"What terrible names
Are 'Jamie' and 'James,'"
Thought Jim.
"'Peter' is sweeter
And 'Patrick' is neater,"

But when he was christened,
Nobody listened
To *him*.

PETER WESLEY-SMITH

PUZZLE

My best friend's name is Billy
But his best friend is Fred
And Fred's is Willy Wiffleson
And Willy's best is Ted.
Ted's best pal is Samuel
While Samuel's is Paul...
It's funny Paul says I'm his best
I hate him most of all.

ARNOLD SPILKA

SOMEONE'S FACE

Someone's face was all frowned shut,
    All squeezed full of grims and crinkles,
Pouts and scowls and gloomers, but
    I could see behind the wrinkles—

Even with her face a-twist,
    I saw Someone peeking through.
And when Someone's nose was kissed,
    Guess who came out giggling—YOU!

JOHN CIARDI